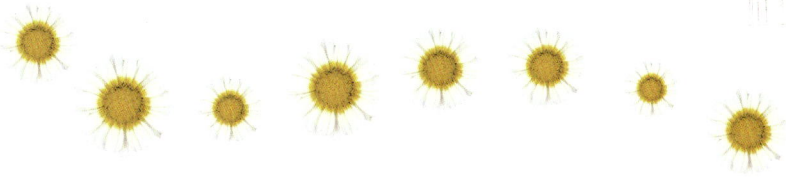

杰作

名著金库

世界的经典

一个孩子的诗园

A Child's Garden of Verses

[英] 罗伯特·路易斯·斯蒂文森 著

刘京 绘

A Child's Garden of Verses

一个孩子的诗园

第十版

文爱艺 译

南方出版传媒

花城出版社

中国·广州

图书在版编目（ＣＩＰ）数据

　　一个孩子的诗园 ／（英）罗伯特·路易斯·斯蒂文森
著；文爱艺译. -- 广州：花城出版社，2019.10
　　（名著金库）
　　ISBN 978-7-5360-8880-1

　　Ⅰ. ①一… Ⅱ. ①罗… ②文… Ⅲ. ①儿童诗歌－诗
集－英国－近代 Ⅳ. ①I561.82

　　中国版本图书馆CIP数据核字(2019)第163193号

出 版 人：肖延兵
责任编辑：陈宾杰　黄玉雯
技术编辑：薛伟民　凌春梅
封面设计：文爱艺

书　　　名 一个孩子的诗园
　　　　　 YI GE HAI ZI DE SHI YUAN
出版发行 花城出版社
　　　　　（广州市环市东路水荫路 11 号）
经　　销 全国新华书店
印　　刷 恒美印务（广州）有限公司
　　　　　（广州南沙经济技术开发区环市大道南路 334 号）
开　　本 787 毫米×1092 毫米　12 开
印　　张 16.5　2 插页
字　　数 120,000 字
版　　次 2019 年 10 月第 1 版　2019 年 10 月第 1 次印刷
定　　价 68.00 元

如发现印装质量问题，请直接与印刷厂联系调换。
购书热线：020 - 37604658　37602954
花城出版社网站：http://www.fcph.com.cn

文爱艺 译

献给爱丽森·坎宁安

——您的孩子呈献

漫漫的长夜，您整夜未眠

为了照顾不懂事的我；

最温暖的您的双手

领着我走过崎岖不平的道路；

为了您曾读过的那些故事书；

为了您曾抚慰过的那些痛楚；

为了您曾给予的怜爱、宽容，

在那些悲喜的日子里——

我的再生之母，我的第一个妻子，

我孩提时代的天使——

收下吧，保姆，收下这本稚嫩的小书，

能唤起人们童年美好回忆和情感的诗集

To ALISON CUNNINGHAM

FROM HER BOY

FOR THE LONG NIGHTS YOU LAY AWAKE
AND WATCHED FOR MY UNWORTHY SAKE:
FOR YOUR MOST COMFORTABLE HAND
THAT LED ME THROUGH THE UNEVEN LAND:
FOR ALL THE STORY BOOKS YOU READ:
FOR ALL THE PAINS YOU COMFORTED:

FOR ALL YOU PITIED, ALL YOU BORE,
IN SAD AND HAPPY DAYS OF YORE—
MY SECOND MOTHER, MY FIRST WIFE,
THE ANGEL OF MY INFANT LIFE—
FROM THE SICK CHILD, NOW WELL AND OLD,
TAKE, NURSE, THE LITTLE BOOK YOU HOLD!

AND GRANT IT, HEAVEN, THAT ALL WHO READ
MAY FIND AS DEAR A NURSE AT NEED,
AND EVERY CHILD WHO LISTS MY RHYME,
IN THE BRIGHT, FIRESIDE, NURSERY CLIME,
MAY HEAR IT IN AS KIND A VOICE
AS MADE MY CHILDISH DAYS REJOICE!

R.L.S.

文爱艺　译

那个原本柔弱的病小孩，如今已经长大！

愿上帝保佑，读过此书的孩子
都能找到一个爱他的保姆，
每个阅读过这些诗篇的孩子，
无论在亮堂堂的炉火边，还是在幼儿园里，
都能够听到同样慈爱的声音
这声音曾使我的童年充满了欢欣！

R.L.S.*

能唤起人们童年美好回忆和情感的诗集

★R.L.S.系罗伯特·路易斯·斯蒂文森的缩写。——译者注

目 录 CONTENTS

A Child's Garden of Verses

一个孩子的诗园

BED IN SUMMER

In winter I get up at night
And dress by yellow candlelight.
In summer, quite the other way,
I have to go to bed by day.

I have to go to bed and see
The birds still hopping on the tree,
Or hear the grown-up people's feet
Still going past me in the street.

And does it not seem hard to you,
When all the sky is clear and blue,
And I should like so much to play,
To have to go to bed by day?

夏天在床上

冬天天没亮我就要起床，
在昏黄的烛光下穿衣裳。
如今夏天变了样，
天没黑我就得上床。

我不得不上床，
眼睁睁看鸟儿还在枝头雀跃，
听着大人们的脚步声，
依然在街道上回响。

这真令人难过，
外面的天空这么晴朗，明亮，
我真想再玩一会儿，
可天没黑我却要上床？

一
个
孩
子
的
诗
园

A THOUGHT

It is very nice to think
The world is full of meat and drink
With little children saying grace
In every Christian kind of place.

A Child's Garden of Verses

奇想

这种想法有多美妙，
世界上到处是肉饼和琼浆，
在每个有基督徒的地方，
孩子们饭前都这样祈祷。

在海边

我漫步在海边，
他们给我一把木铲，
用它来挖沙泥。

我挖的坑像杯子，
每一个都涌进蓝蓝的海水，
直到再也装不下。

AT THE SEASIDE

When I was down beside the sea

A wooden spade they gave to me

To dig the sandy shore.

My holes were empty like a cup,

In every hole the sea came up,

Till it could come no more.

孩子夜里的遐想

妈妈关灯，黑夜来临，
整夜整夜，
我看见一支军队在行进，
就像白天一样清晰。

军队、帝王、将相，
个个手持不同武器，
威风地招摇过市，
白天你从没见过这景象。

即使是草坪上的大马戏团，
也从没表演得这么漂亮；
各种各样的野兽，各种各样的人，
都随着大部队向前行进。

开始，他们慢慢前进，
然后他们越走越快，
我一路紧紧追随着他们，
直到我们一同跌入梦乡。

文爱艺　译

YOUNG NIGHT-THOUGHT

All night long and every night,
When my mamma puts out the light,
I see the people marching by,
As plain as day, before my eye.

Armies and emperors and kings,
All carrying different kinds of things,
And marching in so grand a way,
You never saw the like by day.

So fine a show was never seen
At the great circus on the green:
For every kind of beast and man
Is marching in that caravan.

At first they move a little slow,
But still the faster on they go,
And still beside them close I keep
Until we reach the town of Sleep.

能唤起人们童年
美好回忆和情感的诗集

孩子该做的

孩子应该讲真话，
有人问话要应答，
同桌吃饭要礼貌；
这些努力去做到。

WHOLE DUTY OF CHILDREN

A child should always say what's true,
And speak when he is spoken to,
And behave mannerly at table;
At least as far as he is able.

文爱艺 译

雨

雨呀，到处下，
落在田间，落到树上，
雨点拍打着雨伞，
又落进汪洋中的小船里。

RAIN

The rain is raining all around,
It falls on field and tree,
It rains on the umbrellas here,
And on the ships at sea.

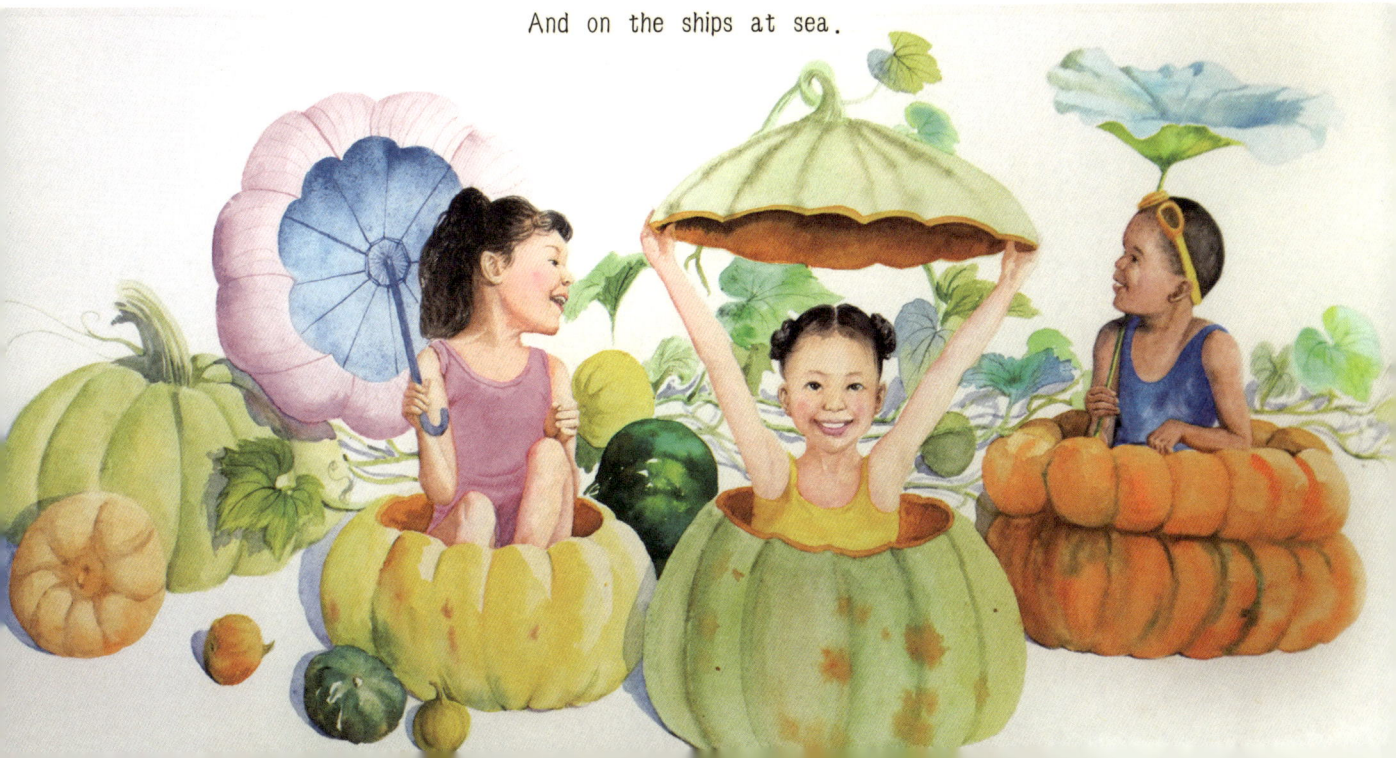

海盗的故事

我们三人，在草地上，荡着秋千，
又从草地上的篮子里钻出来。
春风啊春风，在空气中吹拂，
地上的草波呀，就像那海上翻滚的浪。

今天我们去冒险，船儿驶向何方，
天气将怎样，星星可会指引航向？
风将带着我们飘向非洲，飘向——
普罗维登斯、巴比伦还是马拉巴尔？

嗨！一支舰队横冲过来，
这群草地上怒吼的牛！
快，我们躲开这群疯家伙！
那个小门就是港口，那个花园就是海岸。

文爱艺 译

PIRATE STORY

Three of us afloat in the meadow by the swing,

Three of us aboard in the basket on the lea.

Winds are in the air, they are blowing in the spring,

And waves are on the meadow like the waves there are at sea.

Where shall we adventure, today that we're afloat,

Wary of the weather and steering by a star?

Shall it be to Africa, a-steering of the boat,

To Providence, or Babylon, or off to Malabar?

Hi! But here's a squadron a-rowing on the sea—

Cattle on the meadow a-charging with a roar!

Quick, and we'll escape them, they're as mad as they can be,

The wicket is the harbor and the garden is the shore.

能唤起人们童年美好回忆和情感的诗集

外面的世界

除了小小的我，
谁敢爬上樱桃树？
我双手抱紧树干，
眺望外面的世界。

我看见邻居有一座花园，
美丽的鲜花点缀其间，
还有许多以前从未见过的
奇妙的景观。

我看见河水波光闪闪，
像镜子一样映着蓝天；
只见路上尘土飞扬，
进城人的脚步沉甸甸。

如果我能爬上更高的大树
就能看得更远更远，
远到能看见大河奔流向前，
穿梭船间，奔向大海。

还能看见两边的道路
通向仙境，
那儿所有的孩子都能吃饱，
那儿所有的玩具都会说话。

FOREIGN LANDS

Up into the cherry tree
Who should climb but little me?
I held the trunk with both my hands
And looked abroad on foreign lands.

I saw the next door garden lie,
Adorned with flowers before my eye,
And many pleasant places more
That I had never seen before.

I saw the dimpling river pass
And be the sky's blue looking-glass;
The dusty roads go up and down
With people tramping in to town.

If I could find a higher tree,
Farther and farther I should see,
To where the grown-up river slips
Into the sea among the ships.

To where the roads on either hand
Lead onward into fairy land,
Where all the children dine at five,
And all the playthings come alive.

WINDY NIGHTS

Whenever the moon and stars are set,

Whenever the wind is high,

All night long in the dark and wet

A man goes riding by.

Late in the night, when the fires are out,

Why does he gallop and gallop about?

Whenever the trees are crying aloud,

And ships are tossed at sea,

By, on the highway, low and loud,

By at the gallop goes he.

By at the gallop he goes, and then

By he comes back at the gallop again.

一个孩子的诗园

A Child's Garden of Verses

刮风的夜

月儿悬，星儿闪，
　大风刮不停，
黑夜里，湿气重，
　骑士向前冲，
夜深沉，灯火灭，
为何他总日夜兼程？

树干摇，枝叶响，
　船儿海上漂，
骑士马，一闪过，
　马蹄声声脆，
奔过去，跑回来，
他再一次驰骋归来。

TRAVELS

I should like to rise and go
Where the golden apples grow —
Where below another sky
Parrot islands anchored lie,
And, watched by cockatoos and goats,
Lonely Crusoes building boats —
Where in sunshine reaching out
Eastern cities, miles about,
Are with mosque and minaret
Among sandy gardens set,
And the rich goods from near and far
Hang for sale in the bazaar —
Where the Great Wall round China goes,
And on one side the desert blows,
And with bell and voice and drum,
Cities on the other hum —

文爱艺 译

Where are forests, hot as fire,

Wide as England, tall as a spire,

Full of apes and cocoa-nuts

And the negro hunters' huts —

Where the knotty crocodile

Lies and blinks in the Nile,

And the red flamingo flies

Hunting fish before his eyes —

Where in jungles, near and far,

Man-devouring tigers are,

Lying close and giving ear

Lest the hunt be drawing near,

Or a comer-by be seen

Swinging in a palanquin —

Where among the desert sands

Some deserted city stands,

All its children, sweep and prince,

Grown to manhood ages since,

Not a foot in street or house,

Not a stir of child or mouse,

And when kindly falls the night,

In all the town no spark of light.

There I'll come when I'm a man

With a camel caravan;

Light a fire in the gloom

Of some dusty dining room;

能唤起人们童年

美好回忆和情感的诗集

一个孩子的诗园

A Child's Garden of Verses

See the pictures on the walls,
Heroes, fights and festivals;
And in a corner find the toys
Of the old Egyptian boys.

漫游

文爱艺　译

我真想马上出发
漫游到金苹果生长的地方——
那里有另一片蓝天
鹦鹉岛横卧在海上，
孤独的漂游者在此造船，
鹦鹉和山羊在守候陪伴——
那儿阳光普照
一座座东方小城，清真寺和尖塔点缀，
辽阔的大地上，
庭园矗立，
来自四方的货物在此静候，
等待人们的光顾——
那儿长城环抱着中国，
一侧的荒漠里风沙肆虐，
城市的喧嚣，
钟鼓声回荡在耳畔——
那儿火焰般炎热的森林，
如尖塔般耸立，似英格兰一般广阔，
到处是猴子、椰树
黑人猎手的茅屋随处可见——

那儿鳄鱼披一身鳞甲，
躺在尼罗河里，眨巴着双眼，
还有那红色的火烈鸟，
一见水里的鱼儿，就啄到嘴边——

能唤起人们童年
美好回忆和情感的诗集

那儿丛林密布，
食人的老虎，
卧在附近，竖着耳朵听
怕猎人靠近，
怕有人到林子里来
坐在轿里，摇摇晃晃——
那一片无人的沙地里，
立着一座古城的遗迹，
所有的孩子、扫烟囱的人和王子，
早已经长大成人；
屋里，街上，都没有人走动，
没有孩子笑，也没耗子闹，
当夜晚温和地来临，
全城见不到一丝光亮。
等我长大，我要带着骆驼队
到那儿去；
在幽暗尘封的餐厅
点燃火炬，给周围照明；
看墙上挂着的图画，
看英雄，战斗，节日的欢愉；
最后，我还在角落里发现了
古埃及儿童的一堆玩具。

歌唱

文爱艺　译

鸟儿在树林中筑巢，
歌唱着它们色彩斑驳的蛋；
水手在大海中航行，
歌唱着绳索和货物。

在遥远的日本，孩子们在歌唱，
在西班牙，孩子们也在歌唱；
拉着风琴的风琴手，
在雨中放声歌唱。

SINGING

Of speckled eggs the birdie sings
And nests among the trees;
The sailor sings of ropes and things
In ships upon the seas.

The children sing in far Japan,
The children sing in Spain;
The organ with the organ man
Is singing in the rain.

能唤起人们童年
美好回忆和情感的诗集

一个孩子的诗园

A Child's Garden of Verses

展望未来

当我长大成人，
我会变得强壮，
我就可以骄傲地告诉其他孩子，
不准乱动我的玩具。

LOOKING FORWARD

When I am grown to man's estate
I shall be very proud and great,
And tell the other girls and boys
Not to meddle with my toys.

好玩的游戏

我们用以前卧室的椅子造了艘船，
摆在楼梯上，
装满沙发垫子，
好让它在巨浪中航行。

我们带了锯子和钉子，
还有那装满水的小水桶，
汤姆说："再带个苹果带块蛋糕。"
这些足够维持我们航行到喝下午茶的时候。

我们航行了一天又一天，
愉快极了；
但是汤姆翻船而出，摔伤了膝盖，
最后只剩我一个水手乘风破浪。

A GOOD PLAY

We built a ship upon the stairs
All made of the back-bedroom chairs,
And filled it full of sofa pillows
To go a-sailing on the billows.

We took a saw and several nails,
And water in the nursery pails;
And Tom said, "Let us also take
An apple and a slice of cake" —
Which was enough for Tom and me
To go a-sailing on, till tea.

We sailed along for days and days,
And had the very best of plays;
But Tom fell out and hurt his knee,
So there was no one left but me.

船到哪儿去了？

深棕色的是河，
金黄色的是沙。
河水奔流不息，
两岸树木翠绿。

绿叶飘悠悠，
泡沫像城堡，
我的漂荡的船儿——
何时才到家？

漂过小河，
流过磨坊，
穿越山谷，
绕过山峰。

冲下山涧，
百里之外的地方，
一定有其他的孩子，
带我的小船上岸。

WHERE GO THE BOATS?

Dark brown is the river,
Golden is the sand.
It flows along for ever,
With trees on either hand.

Green leaves a-floating,
Castles of the foam,
Boats of mine a-boating—
Where will all come home?

On goes the river
And out past the mill,
Away down the valley,
Away down the hill.

Away down the river,
A hundred miles or more,
Other little children
Shall bring my boats ashore.

一个孩子的诗园

A Child's Garden of Verses

文爱艺 译

姑姑的裙子

每当姑姑一转身，
她的裙子就会发出奇怪的声响，
身后的裙摆拖在地上，
进门时摇曳生姿。

AUNTIE'S SKIRTS

Whenever Auntie moves around,
Her dresses make a curious sound;
They trail behind her up the floor,
And trundle after through the door.

能唤起人们童年
美好回忆和情感的诗集

THE LAND OF COUNTERPANE

When I was sick and lay a-bed,
I had two pillows at my head,
And all my toys beside me lay
To keep me happy all the day.

And sometimes for an hour or so
I watched my leaden soldiers go,
With different uniforms and drills,
Among the bedclothes, through the hills;

And sometimes sent my ships in fleets
All up and down among the sheets;
Or brought my trees and houses out,
And planted cities all about.

I was the giant great and still
That sits upon the pillow-hill,
And sees before him, dale and plain,
The pleasant land of counterpane.

床单乐园

当我生病躺在床，
头下会垫两个枕头，
所有的玩具都放在身边，
好让我整天都有好心情。

有时候，我会花一两个小时，
观察我的铅制玩具士兵，
看它们穿着不同的制服，
　　拿着不同的武器，
在床上前进，翻越山丘。

有时，我会把我的船编成舰队，
在床单上来回巡视，
或是拿出树木和房屋，
　　四周围上城池。

我就是个伟大的巨人，
平静地坐在枕头山上，
俯视山谷，眺望平原。
多么有趣的床单乐园！

睡梦之乡

从早餐开始，一整天
我都和朋友待在家里，
但每个夜晚我都会外出
直到进入遥远的沉睡之谷。

所有的一切我都只能依靠自己，
没有人告诉我该做什么——
独自一人站在小溪边
独自一人爬上梦的山腰。

那儿有最陌生的东西等着我，
有吃的也有看的，
处处都有令人惊悚的景色
在沉睡谷里游荡直到天亮。

我试着寻找通道，
白天怎么找也找不到，
也不能清楚地记得
我所听到的奇妙乐曲。

THE LAND OF NOD

From breakfast on through all the day
At home among my friends I stay,
But every night I go abroad
Afar into the land of Nod.

All by myself I have to go,
With none to tell me what to do—
All alone beside the streams
And up the mountainsides of dreams.

The strangest things are there for me,
Both things to eat and things to see,
And many frightening sights abroad
Till morning in the land of Nod.

Try as I like to find the way,
I never can get back by day,
Nor can remember plain and clear
The curious music that I hear.

我的影子

我有一个小小的影子，与我须臾不离，
它的魔力超乎想象，
它从头到脚，像极了我，
总是抢先一步，跳上床铺。

最有趣的，是它成长的方式，
不像一般孩子那样慢慢长大，
有时如橡皮球般蹿高，
有时又小到几乎无处寻踪。

好动贪玩，毫无规矩，
设计捣蛋，它最擅长。
你看，它就是一个紧紧跟着我的胆小鬼，
就像黏着保姆一样黏人，真不知羞！

某日清晨，太阳还未露脸，
我起床发现，每棵毛莨都闪着露珠点点，
可我那懒惰的小影子，却像个讨厌的贪睡鬼，
躲在我身后的卧室中，在床上酣酣大睡。

文爱艺 译

MY SHADOW

I have a little shadow that goes in and out with me,
And what can be the use of him is more than I can see.
He is very, very like me from the heels up to the head;
And I see him jump before me, when I jump into my bed.

The funniest thing about him is the way he likes to grow —
Not at all like proper children, which is always very slow;
For he sometimes shoots up taller like an india-rubber ball,
And sometimes gets so little that there's none of him at all.

He hasn't got a notion of how children ought to play,
And can only make a fool of me in every sort of way.
He stays so close beside me, he's a coward you can see;
I'd think shame to stick to nursie as that shadow sticks to me!

One morning very early, before the sun was up,
I rose and found the shining dew on every buttercup;
But my lazy little shadow, like an arrant sleepy-head,
Had stayed at home behind me and was fast asleep in bed.

规则

每个夜晚我都会祈祷，
希望每天都能衣食无忧；
如果我每天都乖乖听话，
饭后会有橘子来奖赏。

一个小孩，又脏又邋遢，
还有很多玩具和零食，
那他一定是个调皮的孩子——
要不然就是他的爸爸跟他一样差劲。

SYSTEM

Every night my prayers I say,
And get my dinner every day;
And every day that I've been good,
I get an orange after food.

The child that is not clean and neat,
With lots of toys and things to eat,
He is a naughty child, I'm sure —
Or else his dear papa is poor.

一个好男孩

我在晨曦中醒来，整日欢欣雀跃，
我从不说脏话，总是微笑，专注地玩耍。

现在太阳终于落到树林之后了，我真高兴，
因为我知道我这一天一直都很乖。

我的床已经铺好，干干净净的，被子光滑又舒适，
我该上床睡觉了，可别忘了祈祷。

我祈求，等明天醒来，我会看到日出，
脑子里没有残留的噩梦，眼前也没有可怕的景象。

只愿一觉睡到天亮，
听画眉鸟在环绕着草坪的丁香树上歌唱。

A GOOD BOY

I woke before the morning, I was happy all the day,
I never said an ugly word, but smiled and stuck to play.

And now at last the sun is going down behind the wood,
And I am very happy, for I know that I've been good.

My bed is waiting cool and fresh, with linen smooth and fair,
And I must off to sleepsin-by, and not forget my prayer.

I know that, till tomorrow I shall see the sun arise,
No ugly dream shall fright my mind, no ugly sight my eyes,

But slumber hold me tightly till I waken in the dawn,
And hear the thrushes singing in the lilacs round the lawn.

床上的美好时光

一个孩子的诗园

A Child's Garden of Verses

灯光从客厅和厨房里映射出来，
穿过窗帘，穿过窗户，穿过隔栏，
天上有成千上万的星星，
高高地在头顶上盘旋着，四处游荡。

树上却不曾有那么多叶子，
教堂和公园也不曾有那么多人，
一群群星星啊，低头看着我，
一群群星星啊，在夜空闪烁。

天狼星，北斗星，猎户星，火星，
还有给水手们指引航向的星，以及其他星座，
它们在天空中闪烁。墙边的木桶里，
一半是水，一半是星星。
大人们还是发现了我，喊着追着我，
把我撵回了床上，
但是星光却一直在我的眼前闪烁，
群星依旧在我的脑海中清晰可见。

ESCAPE AT BEDTIME

The lights from the parlor and kitchen shone out
Through the blinds and the windows and bars;
And high overhead and all moving about,
There were thousands of millions of stars.
There ne'er were such thousands of leaves on a tree,
Nor of people in church or the park,
As the crowds of the stars that looked down upon me,
And that glittered and winked in the dark.

The Dog, and the Plough, and the Hunter, and all
And the Star of the Sailor, and Mars,
These shone in the sky, and the pail by the wall
Would be half full of water and stars.
They saw me at last, and they chased me with cries,
And they soon had me packed into bed;
But the glory kept shining and bright in my eyes,
And the stars going round in my head.

行军曲

拿起梳子，奏起乐章！
向前进，我们来了！
威利戴上了他的苏格兰呢帽，
约翰尼拍打起了他心爱的小鼓。

简·玛丽忙着指挥军队，
彼得负责后勤；
提高警惕，紧急集合，
个个都是精锐士兵！

所有人都威风凛凛，
以双倍的速度向前进；
而小餐布，就像一面旗帜，
骄傲地在木棒上飘扬！

这儿有的是足够的荣耀和战利品，
伟大的司令简！
我们已经巡视完了村庄，
让我们再次荣归故里！

MARCHING SONG

Bring the comb and play upon it!
Marching, here we come!
Willie cocks his highland bonnet,
Johnnie beats the drum.

Mary Jane commands the party,
Peter leads the rear;
Feet in time, alert and hearty,
Each a Grenadier!

All in the most martial manner
Marching double-quick;
While the napkin like a banner
Waves upon the stick!

Here's enough of fame and pillage,
Great commander Jane!
Now that we've been round the village,
Let's go home again.

奶牛

红白相间的温顺奶牛，
我全心全意地喜爱着她：
她使尽全力给我乳汁，
让我吃到苹果馅饼。

在这晴朗的户外，
阳光明媚的白天，
她四处游逛哞哞叫，
但从不会迷路；

任凭风吹雨打，
阵雨淋过，打湿了她，
她却依然漫步在青草丛间，
自在地品尝着牧场上的鲜花。

文爱艺　译

THE COW

The friendly cow all red and white,
I love with all my heart:
She gives me cream with all her might,
To eat with apple tart.

She wanders lowing here and there,
And yet she cannot stray,
All in the pleasant open air,
The pleasant light of day;

And blown by all the winds that pass
And wet with all the showers,
She walks among the meadow grass
And eats the meadow flowers.

能唤起人们童年
美好回忆和情感的诗集

一个孩子的诗园

A Child's Garden of Verses

48 / 49

文爱艺 译

快乐幻想

这个世界充溢着那么多那么多的好东西，
我们呀，都应该都应该像国王一样快乐。

HAPPY THOUGHT

The world is so full of a number of things,
I'm sure we should all be as happy as kings.

能唤起人们童年美好回忆和情感的诗集

一个孩子的诗园

A Child's Garden of Verses

50 / 51

文爱艺 译

风

我看见你牵着风筝高飞，
　　将鸟儿吹向天际；
凡是你到过的地方，
像极了女士穿着裙子走过草地——
　　哦，风儿，你整日吹拂，
　　哦，风儿，你高声歌颂！

我看见你做过很多事情，
　　你却总是如此神秘。
我可以感受到你的力量，听到你的呼喊，
虽然我完全看不见你——
　　哦，风儿，你整日吹拂，
　　哦，风儿，你高声歌颂！

哦，你是如此的强大而冷酷，
哦，风儿，你是年老还是年幼？
你是田间怪物还是丛林野兽，
或者仅仅是比我强壮的孩童？
　　哦，风儿，你整日吹拂，
　　哦，风儿，你高声歌颂！

能唤起人们童年
美好回忆和情感的诗集

THE WIND

I saw you toss the kites on high
And blow the birds about the sky;
And all around I heard you pass,
Like ladies' skirts across the grass —
O wind, a-blowing all day long,
O wind, that sings so loud a song!

I saw the different things you did,
But always you yourself you hid.
I felt you push, I heard you call,
I could not see yourself at all —
O wind, a-blowing all day long,
O wind, that sings so loud a song!

O you that are so strong and cold,
O blower, are you young or old?
Are you a beast of field and tree,
Or just a stronger child than me?
O wind, a-blowing all day long,
O wind, that sings so loud a song!

磨坊纪念品

偷爬围墙，这是个不可饶恕的错误，
折断树枝，爬行向前，
穿过花园墙洞，
一直走到河边。

这儿有个磨坊，嗡嗡声响如雷，
这儿有座堤坝，波浪涌起泡沫，
这儿还有水闸，竞相奔腾赛跑——
虽然离家近了点儿，可这是多么美妙神奇的地方啊！

村庄里的声响逐渐趋于沉寂，
就连小山丘上的鸟儿也默不作声；
磨坊主的双眼满是灰尘模糊不清，
他辛勤地劳作着，听不见外面的声音。

时光流逝，磨轮却依旧伫立在河边，
今天它依然为孩子们转动着，
旋转着，飞奔着，咆哮着，扬着泡沫，
直到所有的男孩都离开了，依旧永不停息。

某一天，从西印度群岛和海上回到家，
那些士兵和英雄，
会发现老磨坊的车轮依旧转动着，
翻转搅打着河水，扬着泡沫，永不停息。

你拿着的，是我在争吵后给你的豆子，
而我拿着的，是你在星期六给我的玻璃球，
如今我俩都已年迈，身着荣装。
就让我们在这儿重聚，缅怀那过往的时光。

KEEPSAKE MILL

Over the borders, a sin without pardon,
Breaking the branches and crawling below,
Out through the breach in the wall of the garden,
Down by the banks of the river, we go.

Here is the mill with the humming of thunder,
Here is the weir with the wonder of foam,
Here is the sluice with the race running under —
Marvelous places, though handy to home!

Sounds of the village grow stiller and stiller,
Stiller the note of the birds on the hill;
Dusty and dim are the eyes of the miller,
Deaf are his ears with the moil of the mill.

Years may go by, and the wheel in the river
Wheel as it wheels for us children, today,
Wheel and keep roaring and foaming for ever
Long after all of the boys are away.

Home from the Indies and home from the ocean,
Heroes and soldiers we all shall come home;
Still we shall find the old mill wheel in motion,
Turning and churning that river to foam.

You with the bean that I gave when we quarreled,
I with your marble of Saturday last,
Honored and old and all gaily appareled,
Here we shall meet and remember the past.

GOOD AND BAD CHILDREN

Children, you are very little,
And your bones are very brittle;
If you would grow great and stately,
You must try to walk sedately.

You must still be bright and quiet,
And content with simple diet;
And remain, through all bewild'ring,
Innocent and honest children.

Happy hearts and happy faces,
Happy play in grassy places—
That was how, in ancient ages,
Children grew to kings and sages.

But the unkind and the unruly,
And the sort who eat unduly,
They must never hope for glory—
Theirs is quite a different story!

Cruel children, crying babies,
All grow up as geese and gabies,
Hated, as their age increases,
By their nephews and their nieces.

好孩子和坏孩子

孩子们，你们还这么小，
　骨头都还没长结实呢，
如果你想长得又高又壮，
那么行走时你一定要尽量稳重。

你还要机灵点，安静点，
　不挑剔食物，
还要记得在困惑面前，
做一个天真诚实的孩子。

愉快的心情，愉快的笑容，
　在草场上欢乐地嬉闹——
在古时候，孩子们都是这样，
从儿童慢慢成为国王和圣贤。

那些不友善的，任性的，
　吃东西挑三拣四的，
他们休想得到荣誉——
他们的人生将会完全不同。

残忍的孩子，爱哭的宝宝，
　长大了也只会变成傻瓜，
随着年龄的增长，
甚至会被自己的晚辈所厌恶。

外国的小孩

印第安、苏族和克罗族的小朋友，
　生活在严寒中的因纽特小朋友，
　　土耳其和日本的小朋友们，
　　哦！难道你们不希望跟我一样？

　　你们见过绯红的树木，
　　　和海边的狮子；
　　你们吃过鸵鸟下的蛋，
　　也曾把乌龟掀了个四脚朝天。

　　这样的生活非常好，
　　但是没有我的惬意舒适啊；
　　你们踢踢踏踏走路的时候，
　　一定常常厌倦不身在国外。

　　你们有奇特的东西吃，
　　　而我只吃日常的肉；
　　你们要在泡沫外面居住，
　　可我住在家里安全又舒适。

印第安、苏族和克罗族的小朋友，
　生活在严寒中的因纽特小朋友，
　　土耳其和日本的小朋友们，
　　哦！难道你们不希望跟我一样？

文爱艺 译

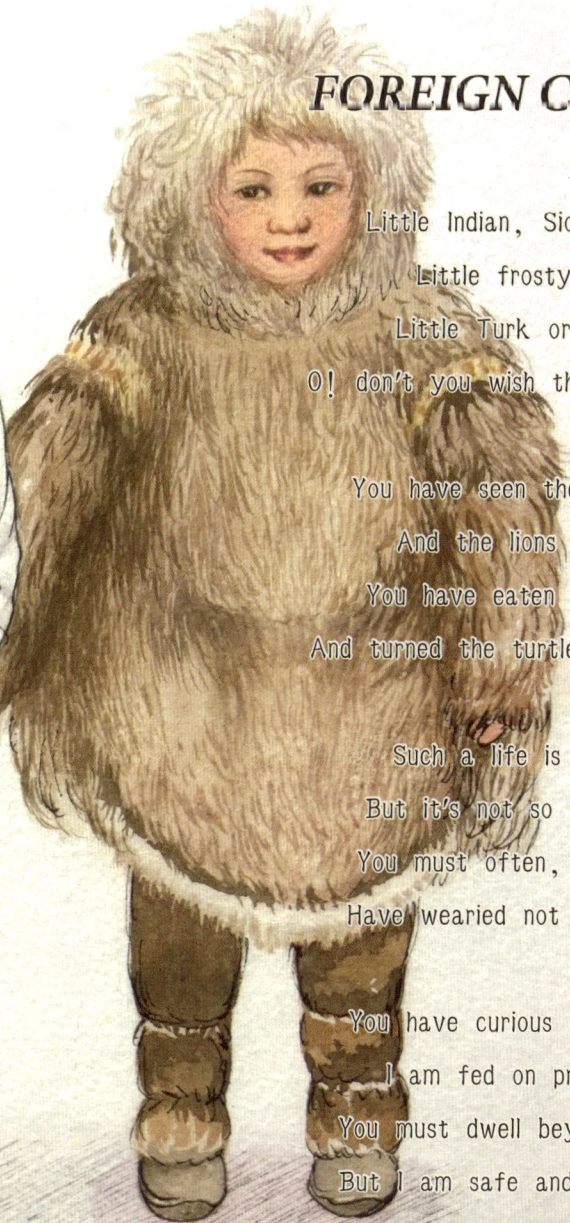

FOREIGN CHILDREN

Little Indian, Sioux or Crow,

Little frosty Eskimo,

Little Turk or Japanese,

O! don't you wish that you were me?

You have seen the scarlet trees

And the lions over seas;

You have eaten ostrich eggs,

And turned the turtles off their legs.

Such a life is very fine,

But it's not so nice as mine:

You must often, as you trod,

Have wearied not to be abroad.

You have curious things to eat,

I am fed on proper meat;

You must dwell beyond the foam,

But I am safe and live at home.

Little Indian, Sioux or Crow,

Little frosty Eskimo,

Little Turk or Japanese,

Oh! Don't you wish that you were me?

能唤起人们童年
美好回忆和情感的诗集

太阳之旅

太阳从不休息，
哪怕晚上我睡觉的时候，
它仍然按它的方式绕着地球，
日复一日地运转。

在阳光灿烂的日子里，
我们在暖暖的花园里尽情玩耍，
一个个贪睡的小小印第安人，
被香香地亲吻过之后就都被抱去床上了。

而当我喝完下午茶去玩的时候，
大西洋彼岸正是拂晓时分。
所有西方的孩子，
正起床，穿衣戴帽。

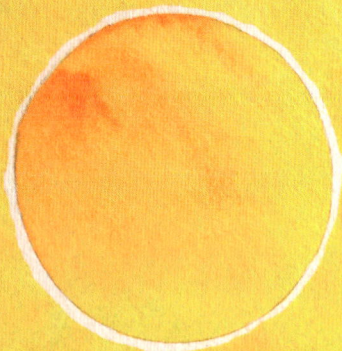

文爱艺　译

THE SUN 'S TRAVELS

The sun is not a-bed, when I
At night upon my pillow lie;
Still round the earth his way he takes,
And morning after morning makes.

While here at home, in shining day,
We round the sunny garden play,
Each little Indian sleepyhead
Is being kissed and put to bed.

And when at eve I rise from tea,
Day dawns beyond the Atlantic Sea,
And all the children in the West
Are getting up and being dressed.

能唤起人们童年
美好回忆和情感的诗集

点灯人

茶将沏，日已落，
是时候趴在窗上守候着灯夫李瑞经过了；
每晚，饮茶时分，人未坐定，
他就会扛着梯子提着灯笼从街上经过。

汤姆想成为司机，玛丽亚想去航海，
我的爸爸是位银行家，要多富就有多富；
而我，当我长大后，当我可以自己做主时，
哦，李瑞，我会跟着你每晚四处去点灯！

我们是多么幸运啊，门口有盏灯。
你点了那么多灯，停下来休息一下吧！
哦，当你扛着梯子，提着灯笼，匆匆而过的时候，
李瑞啊，请看看身旁的这个小孩儿，
并向他点头示意！

8

THE LAMPLIGHTER

My tea is nearly ready and the sun has left the sky;
It's time to take the window to see Leerie going by;
For every night at teatime and before you take your seat,
With lantern and with ladder he comes posting up the street.

Now Tom would be a driver and Maria go to sea,
And my papa's a banker and as rich as he can be;
But I, when I am stronger and can choose what I'm to do,
O Leerie, I'll go round at night and light the lamps with you!

For we are very lucky, with a lamp before the door.
And Leerie stops to light it as he lights so many more;
And O! before you hurry by with ladder and with light,
O Leerie, see a little child and nod to him tonight!

我的床是条船

我的床像一条小船，
保姆扶我踏上船儿，
她给我穿上水手衣服，
送我在黑暗中起航。

夜里，我走上甲板，
向岸上的朋友们道别；
我闭上双眼起航远行，
什么也听不见看不见。

有时我会带些东西上床，
就像细心的水手一样，
或许是一小块婚宴蛋糕，
或许是一两个玩具。

我们整晚在黑暗中航行，
当白天最终来临时，
我却发现我的船儿，
安稳地停靠在我的房间。

文爱艺 译

MY BED IS A BOAT

My bed is like a little boat;
Nurse helps me in when I embark;
She girds me in my sailor's coat
And starts me in the dark.

At night, I go on board and say
Good-night to all my friends on shore;
I shut my eyes and sail away
And see and hear no more.

And sometimes things to bed I take,
As prudent sailors have to do:
Perhaps a slice of wedding cake,
Perhaps a toy or two.

All night across the dark we steer:
But when the day returns at last,
Safe in my room, beside the pier,
I find my vessel fast.

THE MOON

The moon has a face like the clock in the hall;
She shines on thieves on the garden wall,
On streets and fields and harbor quays,
And birdies asleep in the forks of the trees.

The squalling cat and the squeaking mouse,
The howling dog by the door of the house,
The bat that lies in bed at noon,
All love to be out by the light of the moon.

But all of the things that belong to the day
Cuddle to sleep to be out of her way;
And flowers and children close their eyes
Till up in the morning the sun shall arise.

文爱艺 译

月亮

月亮的脸，像礼堂里的时钟，
月光洒在花园围墙的小偷身上，
还有街上，田间，海港码头上，
还洒在树杈间沉沉入睡的鸟儿们身上。

喵喵叫的猫，鬼鬼祟祟作祟的老鼠，
还有把门汪汪叫的狗儿，
日上三竿还挂在床上的蝙蝠，
它们都喜欢在月光下活动。

可是白天活动的小生物们，
只能在夜晚蜷曲着睡去，
花儿和孩子们闭上他们的眼睛，
直待到拂晓时分太阳升起。

能唤起人们童年
美好回忆和情感的诗集

秋千

你喜不喜欢荡秋千，
荡着秋千飞上蓝天？
哦，我觉得在小孩子的世界，
这是最快乐的玩耍！

飞向空中，越过围墙，
我看到天地如此宽广，
河流，树木，牛群和所有的一切，
勾画着这美丽的乡村——

我低头看见绿葱葱的花园，
脚下面还有棕色的屋顶——
我荡着秋千又飞上天，
飞上飞下不厌倦！

THE SWING

How do you like to go up in a swing,
Up in the air so blue?
Oh, I do think it the pleasantest thing
Ever a child can do!

Up in the air and over the wall,
Till I can see so wide,
Rivers and trees and cattle and all
Over the countryside —

Till I look down on the garden green,
Down on the roof so brown —
Up in the air I go flying again,
Up in the air and down!

该起床啦

一只黄嘴鸟，
单脚在窗台上跳呀跳，
瞪着明亮的眼睛喳喳叫：
"还在睡懒觉，害臊不害臊？"

TIME TO RISE

A birdie with a yellow bill
Hopped upon the window sill,
Cocked his shining eye and said:
"Ain't you 'shamed, you sleepyhead?"

明镜河

河水静静地流淌，
层层涟漪、水波荡漾——
啊，光洁的石子，
啊，平滑的溪流！

落花顺着水流漂去，银鱼在溪中畅游，
平静的河水呀，像蓝天般清澈——
孩子是多么地渴望啊，
能在这水里玩个够！

我们能看到自己红润的脸庞，
倒映在流动的溪水中摇晃，
漂到凉爽的地方，
幽暗又清凉！

直到风儿将水面吹皱，
溅湿了貂鼠，乐坏了鳟鱼，
水波渐渐散去，
已消失得无处寻踪。

看，光圈互相追逐，交相辉映；
水下变成漆黑的夜晚，
就像是妈妈，
把灯全都吹灭那般！

耐心一点儿、孩子们，就一会儿——
等到涟漪的水纹散去；
水中的一切，
就又都会重回清澈。

LOOKING-GLASS RIVER

文爱艺　译

Smooth it slides upon its travel,
Here a wimple, there a gleam —
O the clean gravel!
O the smooth stream!

Sailing blossoms, silver fishes,
Paven pools as clear as air —
How a child wishes
To live down there!

We can see our colored faces
Floating on the shaken pool
Down in cool places
Dim and very cool;

Till a wind or water wrinkle,
Dipping marten, plumping trout,
Spreads in a twinkle
And blots all out.

See the rings pursue each other;
All below grows black as night,
Just as if mother
Had blown out the light!

Patience, children, just a minute —
See the spreading circles die;
The stream and all in it
Will clear by-and-by.

美味的面包

过来这儿，哦，我的小脏孩儿们，
　　这儿有美味的面包，
　　就在我的起居室里，
　　孩子们哪，你们快来尝尝，
在这透着金黄色香气的金雀花丛中，
　　　在这松树的树荫下，
　　　当美美地饱餐之后，
乖乖听我给你们讲神话故事。

文爱艺 译

FAIRY BREAD

Come up here, O dusty feet!
Here is fairy bread to eat.
Here in my retiring room,
Children, you may dine
On the golden smell of broom
And the shade of pine;
And when you have eaten well,
Fairy stories hear and tell.

能唤起人们童年
美好回忆和情感的诗集

从火车上往外看

比精灵还快，比巫师更疾，
越过大桥和房屋，跨过树篱和沟渠；
向前冲，像是战火中的军队，
穿过牧场，穿过马群，穿过牛群；
山川起伏，平原辽阔，
飞逝而过如倾盆大雨；
突然，一眨眼的工夫，
新漆的车站也呼啸而过。

这儿有个小孩儿，胡乱攀爬，
独自一人采摘黑莓；
这儿有个流浪汉，呆呆地站在一边，
凝望着，
那边还有大片绿油油的连串的雏菊花！
路边还有策马扬鞭疾行的大马车，
车上坐着人，载着货；
这头一个磨坊，那头一条小河：
都只匆匆一瞥，别后就一去不返！

文爱艺　译

FROM A RAILWAY CARRIAGE

Faster than fairies, faster than witches,
Bridges and houses, hedges and ditches;
And charging along like troops in a battle,
All through the meadows the horses and cattle:
All of the sights of the hill and the plain
Fly as thick as driving rain;
And ever again, in the wink of an eye,
Painted stations whistle by.

Here is a child who clambers and scrambles,
All by himself and gathering brambles;
Here is a tramp who stands and gazes;
And there is the green for stringing the daisies!
Here is a cart run away in the road
Lumping along with man and load;
And here is a mill and there is a river:
Each a glimpse and gone forever!

能唤起人们童年美好回忆和情感的诗集

WINTERTIME

Late lies the wintry sun a-bed,
A frosty, fiery sleepyhead;
Blinks but an hour or two; and then,
A blood-red orange, sets again.

Before the stars have left the skies,
At morning in the dark I rise;
And shivering in my nakedness,
By the cold candle, bathe and dress.

Close by the jolly fire I sit
To warm my frozen bones a bit;
Or, with a reindeer-sled, explore
The colder countries round the door.

When to go out, my nurse doth wrap
Me in my comforter and cap:
The cold wind burns my face, and blows
Its frosty pepper up my nose.

Black are my steps on silver sod,
Thick blows my frosty breath abroad;
And tree and house, and hill and lake,
Are frosted like a wedding cake.

冬日时光

冬日的太阳爱睡懒觉，
是个冷漠暴躁的家伙，
只执勤一两个小时，然后
就用血红的晚霞再度把天空布满。

在星星离开天空之前，
天还没亮我就得起来；
哆嗦着光溜溜的身子，
借着冰冷的烛光，沐浴着装。

紧紧地挨着壁炉坐下，
给冻僵了的身子骨取取暖；
或是带着驯鹿雪橇，去探索
门外更严寒的国度。

出门时，保姆会把我裹好，
我围着围巾戴着暖帽，
寒风迎面而来，吹冻着脸庞，
冰冷的雪片扭捏着我的鼻子。

银色的草地皮上有我黑黑的脚印，
寒风将我冰冷的呼吸吹到远方；
树木啊，房子啊，还有山丘和湖泊，
都冻成了一块婚礼蛋糕！

干草棚

在整个快乐的草原上，
　绿草长到齐肩高，
　闪光的镰刀快又宽，
　割下青草去晒干。

　散发着香气的青草，
　装上马车运回家，
　在这儿堆成山一样高，
　让登山的人来往上爬。

　这儿是清凉山，荒疏峰，
那儿是老鹰崖，擎天岭——
　居住在这里的老鼠，
　也没我那么幸福！

　爬上草堆多高兴，
这里真是一个玩乐的好地方，
　甜蜜，昏暗，灰尘弥漫空中，
　我爱快乐的干草山！

文爱艺 译

THE HAYLOFT

Through all the pleasant meadow-side
The grass grew shoulder-high,
Till the shining scythes went far and wide
And cut it down to dry.

These green and sweetly smelling crops
They led in wagons home;
And they piled them here in mountaintops
For mountaineers to roam.

Here is Mount Clear, Mount Rusty-Nail,
Mount Eagle and Mount High; —
The mice that in these mountains dwell,
No happier are than I!

O what a joy to clamber there,
O what a place for play,
With the sweet, the dim, the dusty air,
The happy hills of hay.

能唤起人们童年美好回忆和情感的诗集

告别农场

马车终于停在了门口；
急切的孩子们，抢着上马车，
挥手告别，齐声高唱：
别了，别了，所有的一切！

别了，房子和花园，田野和草坪，
牧场的大门——我们曾经的秋千，
别了，水泵和马厩，树木和秋千，
别了，别了，所有的一切！

永远地告别了，
哦，干草棚门上的梯子，
哦，布满蜘蛛网的草棚，
别了，别了，所有的一切！

挥动马鞭，就此离去；
树木和房子在视线里渐渐变小；
终于，我们在森林边拐弯了；
别了，别了，所有的一切！

文爱艺 译

FAREWELL TO THE FARM

The coach is at the door at last;
The eager children, mounting fast
And kissing hands, in chorus sing:
Good-bye, good-bye, to everything!

To house and garden, field and lawn,
The meadow-gates we swang upon,
To pump and stable, tree and swing,
Good-bye, good-bye, to everything!

And fare you well for evermore,
O ladder at the hayloft door,
O hayloft , where the cobwebs cling,
Good-bye, good-bye, to everything!

Crack goes the whip, and off we go;
The trees and houses smaller grow;
Last, round the woody turn we swing:
Good-bye, good-bye, to everything!

能唤起人们童年
美好回忆和情感的诗集

NORTH-WEST PASSAGE

西北之行

1. 晚安

当明亮的煤油灯被点亮，
夜晚的时光又开始了……
万籁俱寂，在田野，在小巷，
神秘的夜晚重又降临。

我们盯着将要燃尽的余灰，
在炉火燃烧的壁炉前，
我们的脸就像被涂过了颜色一样，
就像投影在玻璃窗上的图像。

我们真的要上床去了吗？那好吧，
让我们起身，像大人一样。
迈着勇敢的步伐去面对
通往床那边的漫长幽暗的旅程。

再会了，哥哥姐姐们，还有爸爸妈妈！
再会了，快乐的炉火旁的欢聚！
你唱的歌，你讲的童话，
只有到遥远的明天才能再见了！

1. GOOD NIGHT

文爱艺 译

When the bright lamp is carried in,
The sunless hours again begin;
O'er all without, in field and lane,
The haunted night returns again.

Now we behold the embers flee
About the firelit hearth; and see
Our faces painted as we pass,
Like pictures, on the window-glass.

Must we to bed indeed? Well then,
Let us arise and go like men,
And face with an undaunted tread
The long, black passage up to bed.

Farewell, O brother, sister, sire!
O pleasant party round the fire!
The songs you sing, the tales you tell,
Till far tomorrow, fare ye well!

能唤起人们童年美好回忆和情感的诗集

2. SHADOW MARCH

All round the house is the jet black night;
It stares through the windowpane;
It crawls in the corners, hiding from the light,
And it moves with the moving flame.

Now my little heart goes a-beating like a drum,
With the breath of the Bogie in my hair;
And all round the candle the crooked shadows come
And go marching along up the stair.

The shadow of the balusters, the shadow of the lamp,
The shadow of the child that goes to bed—
All the wicked shadows coming, tramp, tramp, tramp,
With the black night overhead.

文爱艺 译

2. 影中漫行

整个屋子都笼罩在漆黑的夜色中，
它透过玻璃窗徐徐而来；
它在角落里葡匐，躲避着光亮，
它随着移动的火焰飘浮。

现在我小小的心脏如击鼓般跳动着，
恐怖的气息在发梢间游弋着；
绕着蜡烛，扭曲的影子出现了，
慢慢地沿楼梯上楼。

栏杆的影子，灯具的影子，
上床睡觉的小孩儿的影子，
所有邪恶的影子一拥而来，
大步前进，啪、啪、啪……
在黑暗的上空盘旋。

能唤起人们童年
美好回忆和情感的诗集

3. 在港内

终于，到了我的卧室，
我害怕的脚步声嗒嗒地逼近，
迫切地从又冷又昏暗的外面，
钻到我又暖又快乐的小屋里。

在那儿，安全抵达后，我们转身，
将尾随的影子拒之门外，
最后关上愉悦的大门，
忘却所有经历的危难。

然后，当妈妈来到床边，
她一定是踮着脚进来的，
看着我暖暖地入眠，
进入了沉睡的乐园。

文爱艺 译

3. IN PORT

Last, to the chamber where I lie
My fearful footsteps patter nigh,
And come from out the cold and gloom
Into my warm and cheerful room.

There, safe arrived, we turn about
To keep the coming shadows out,
And close the happy door at last
On all the perils that we past.

Then, when mamma goes by to bed,
She shall come in with tiptoe tread,
And see me lying warm and fast
And in the Land of Nod at last.

能唤起人们童年

美好回忆和情感的诗集

THE CHILD ALONE

孤独的孩子

隐形玩伴

当孩子们在草地上独自玩耍，
隐形玩伴就会来到身旁，
当孩子们快乐、寂寞又听话时，
隐形玩伴便从林间悄然而至。

没人听得见，也没人看得见，
他是一幅你永远描摹不出的画，
但他是存在的，无论在户外还是在家，
当孩子们开心而又独自玩耍着的时候。

月桂林中小憩，青草地上飞驰，
叮咚的乐声从音乐盒中飞洒，
他便和声浅吟低唱，
无论何时，当你快乐，又不知为何，
那他一定就在你身旁！

他喜欢自己小小的，讨厌长大，
这就是他，栖息在你挖的山洞里，
这就是他，当你和小锡兵玩的时候，
他总是站在法国那边，尽管屡战屡败。

这就是他，露重更深时，
他哄你酣然入睡，远离烦恼。
不管他身在何方，在碗柜里或是架子上，
都会将你的玩具好好照料！

THE UNSEEN PLAYMATE

When children are playing alone on the green,
In comes the playmate that never was seen.
When children are happy and lonely and good,
The Friend of the Children comes out of the wood.

Nobody heard him and nobody saw,
His is a picture you never could draw.
But he's sure to be present, abroad or at home,
When children are happy and playing alone.

He lies in the laurels, he runs on the grass,
He sings when you tinkle the musical glass;
Whene'er you are happy and cannot tell why,
The Friend of the Children is sure to be by!

He loves to be little, he hates to be big,
'Tis he that inhabits the caves that you dig;
'Tis he when you play with your soldiers of tin
That sides with the Frenchmen and never can win.

'Tis he, when at night you go off to your bed,
Bids you go to sleep and not trouble your head;
For wherever they're lying, in cupboard or shelf,
'Tis he will take care of your playthings himself!

我和我的船

现在我正是这条整洁小船的船长，
让我的船在池塘上漂一会儿，再让它四处漂荡；
等我长大点后，就要去寻找那秘密，
到那时我就知道
怎样让我的小船儿扬帆远航。

我想长到像船舵里的玩具娃娃那么小，
然后让玩具娃娃活蹦乱跳，
有了他这个助手，我就要去航行，
航行到海上，沐浴那快乐的海风，
我的小船，乘风破浪。

噢，你看，我穿过激流，驶过芦苇荡，
你听，激流在船头欢笑，
有了娃娃水手的陪伴，我将探险远航，
去他们以前没去过的岛屿，
还要燃放一便士买来的大炮。

MY SHIP AND I

文爱艺 译

O it's I that am the captain of a tidy little ship,
Of a ship that goes a-sailing on the pond;
And my ship it keeps a-turning all around and all about;
But when I'm a little older, I shall find the secret out
How to send my vessel sailing on beyond.

For I mean to grow as little as the dolly at the helm,
And the dolly I intend to come alive;
And with him beside to help me, it's a-sailing I shall go,
It's a-sailing on the water, when the jolly breezes blow,
And the vessel goes a divie-divie dive.

O it's then you'll see me sailing through the rushes and the reeds,
And you'll hear the water singing at the prow;
For beside the dolly sailor, I'm to voyage and explore,
To land upon the island where no dolly was before,
And to fire the penny cannon in the bow.

我的王国

沿着流淌的小河而下，
我发现了一个小幽谷，
还不到我头的高度。
石楠花和荆豆正含苞待放，
在夏日里散发迷人的芬芳，
有黄色的也有红色的。

我称小水塘为大海，
这个小幽谷对我来说很大。
因为我是如此渺小。
我造了条船，我建了座城，
我上上下下搜寻着大洞穴，
并且给它们一一命名。

我宣布，所有的一切都是我的，
空中飞的小麻雀是我的，
水中游的小鲦鱼是我的，
这就是整个世界，而我就是国王；
蜜蜂来到这儿为我歌唱，
燕子来到这儿为我起舞。

文爱艺　译

再也没有比这儿更深的海了，
也没有比这儿更宽的平原了，
我是这里唯一的国王。
最后我听到妈妈叫唤我，
日落时分站在门外，
唤我回去吃饭。

我不得不起身离开我的幽谷，
离开我的泛着涟漪的泉水，
离开含苞待放的石楠花。
天哪，当我快要到家时，
保姆突然如庞然大物站在面前，
我的房间是如此宽阔如此凉爽！

能唤起人们童年
美好回忆和情感的诗集

MY KINGDOM

Down by a shining water well
I found a very little dell,
No higher than my head.
The heather and the gorse about
In summer bloom were coming out,
Some yellow and some red.

I called the little pool a sea;
The little hills were big to me;
For I am very small.
I made a boat, I made a town,
I searched the caverns up and down,
And named them one and all.

And all about was mine, I said,
The little sparrows overhead,
Thc littlc minnow3 too.

A Child's Garden of Verses

文爱艺 译

This was the world and I was king;
For me the bees came by to sing,
    For me the swallows flew.

I played there were no deeper seas,
Nor any wider plains than these,
    Nor other kings than me.
At last I heard my mother call
Out from the house at evenfall,
    To call me home to tea.

And I must rise and leave my dell,
And leave my dimpled water well,
    And leave my heather blooms.
Alas! and as my home I neared,
How very big my nurse appeared,
    How great and cool the rooms!

能唤起人们童年
美好回忆和情感的诗集

冬日里的连环画

夏天逝去，冬日降临——
严寒的晨曦，拇指瑟瑟发抖，
窗边的知更鸟，冬日里的白嘴鸦，
还有一本本好看的连环画。

水流冻成了冰川，
保姆和我能够在上面行走；
但我们还是能看到流淌着的溪水，
就在那一本本好看的连环画里。

所有美好的事物都在书上，
等着孩子们来瞧看。
羊群和牧羊人，树木和枝丫。
就在那一本本好看的连环画里。

我们能看到各种各样的东西，
大海和城市，或远或近的，
还有飞舞中的精灵，
就在那一本本好看的连环画里。

我该怎样歌颂赞美你呢，
那些快乐的炉火缭绕的日子，
安稳地坐在乐园的角落里，
阅读那一本本好看的连环画。

PICTURE-BOOKS IN WINTER

Summer fading, Winter comes —
Frosty mornings, tingling thumbs,
Window robins, Winter rooks,
And the picture storybooks.

Water now is turned to stone
Nurse and I can walk upon;
Still we find the flowing brooks
In the picture story-books.

All the pretty things put by,
Wait upon the children's eye,
Sheep and shepherds, trees and crooks,
In the picture storybooks.

We may see how all things are,
Seas and cities, near and far,
And the flying fairies' looks,
In the picture story-books.

How am I to sing your praise,
Happy chimney-corner days,
Sitting safe in nursery nooks,
Reading picture story books?

我的珍宝

我把那些栗子藏在鸟窝的后面，
那也是我的锡制玩具兵休息的地方。
那是秋天里我和保姆一起采来的，
在海边流着泉水的树林里。

这个哨子（声音是多么清脆！），
是我们在田地的那一边操场的尽头做的。
用我的小刀和一根树枝做成的，
这全是保姆一人的功劳！

这石头，有白色、黄色还有灰色，
我都说不清是在多远的地方发现的。
尽管又累又冷，我还是带它们回家了，
虽然爸爸对它们不屑一顾，我却相信它们就是金子。

在我所有的财宝中，最后一个是国王，
因为很少有孩子能拥有这样一件瑰宝；
那是一把凿子，有柄有刃，
这定是真正的木匠的大作！

MY TREASURES

These nuts, that I keep in the back of the nest,
Where all my tin soldiers are lying at rest,
Were gathered in Autumn by nursie and me
In a wood with a well by the side of the sea.

This whistle we made (and how clearly it sounds!)
By the side of a field at the end of the grounds.
Of a branch of a plane, with a knife of my own, —
It was nursie who made it, and nursie alone!

The stone, with the white and the yellow and grey,
We discovered I cannot tell how far away;
And I carried it back although weary and cold,
For though father denies it,
I'm sure it is gold.

But of all of my treasures the last is the king,
For there's very few children possess such a thing;
And that is a chisel, both handle and blade,
Which a man who was really a carpenter made.

木头城

你能用积木搭出什么样儿的建筑？
城堡和宫殿，寺庙和码头。
雨可能下个不停，其他人都出去玩了，
而我是快乐的，在家里造着我的大房子。

沙发做山脉，地毯当海洋，
我要在那儿建造自己的城堡：
一座苏格兰教堂，一座磨坊，还有一座宫殿矗立在旁，
再添一个港口，供我的小船停靠。

雄伟的宫殿，有柱子和围墙，
还有宝塔屹立在顶端，
台阶整整齐齐地排下来，
通往停泊着小船的避风港。

这只是要远航的，那只就此停靠，
听甲板上水手在歌唱，
看吧，我宫殿的阶梯上，那国王们，
带着礼物来来往往！

现在我玩够了，让它倒塌吧！
一瞬间塔就倒了，
一块块积木自由地散落了一地，
海边的城市还剩下些什么？

然而当我细看时，我还能看到，
苏格兰教堂和宫殿，船只和行人，
只要我活着，不管身处何方，
我将永远惦记着我的海边城堡！

BLOCK CITY

What are you able to build with your blocks?
Castles and palaces, temples and docks.
Rain may keep raining, and others go roam,
But I can be happy and building at home.

Let the sofa be mountains, the carpet be sea,
There I'll establish a city for me:
A kirk and a mill and a palace beside,
And a harbor as well where my vessels may ride.

Great is the palace with pillar and wall,
A sort of a tower on the top of it all,
And steps coming down in an orderly way
To where my toy vessels lie safe in the bay.

This one is sailing and that one is moored:
Hark to the song of the sailors on board!
And see on the steps of my palace, the kings
Coming and going with presents and things!

Now I have done with it, down let it go!
All in a moment the town is laid low.
Block upon block lying scattered and free,
What is there left of my town by the sea?

Yet as I saw it, I see it again,
The kirk and the palace, the ships and the men,
And as long as I live and where'er I may be,
I'll always remember my town by the sea.

故事书之都

黄昏时分，点亮了灯，
爸爸妈妈围着炉火而坐，
他们在家聊天，唱歌，
其他什么都不玩。

现在，我拿着我的小枪，匍匐着，
　　躲在黑暗的墙边，
　　绕过森林小径，
　　藏在沙发后面。

在夜里，　那儿没有人能发现，
　　我独自一人躺在猎人营里，
　　玩耍着那些读过的书，
　　　直到上床睡觉。

这些是山丘，那些是森林，
这便是我布满星星的秘密基地，
　　那儿还有条河流，
　　咆哮的狮子前来饮水。

我还看到了远处的其他人，
好像躺在点着灯的帐篷里，
而我，就像是印度侦察员，
　　潜伏在他们的派对里。

因此，当保姆来寻我时，
　　我穿过大海回家，
　　恋恋不舍地爬上床去，
躺进我亲爱的故事书之都里。

THE LAND OF STORYBOOKS

At evening, when the lamp is lit,
Around the fire my parents sit;
They sit at home and talk and sing,
And do not play at anything.

Now, with my little gun, I crawl
All in the dark along the wall,
And follow round the forest track
Away behind the sofa back.

There, in the night, where none can spy,
All in my hunter's camp I lie,
And play at books that I have read
Till it is time to go to bed.

These are the hills, these are the woods,
These are my starry solitudes;
And there the river by whose brink
The roaring lions come to drink.

I see the others far away
As if in firelit camp they lay,

文爱艺 译

And I, like to an Indian scout,
Around their party prowled about.

So, when my nurse comes in for me,
Home I return across the sea,
And go to bed with backward looks
At my dear land of Storybooks.

ARMIES IN THE FIRE

The lamps now glitter down the street;
Faintly sound the falling feet;
And the blue even slowly falls
About the garden trees and walls.

Now in the falling of the gloom
The red fire paints the empty room:
And warmly on the roof it looks,
And flickers on the backs of books.

Armies march by tower and spire
Of cities blazing, in the fire;
Till as I gaze with staring eyes,
The armies fade, the lustre dies.

Then once again the glow returns;
Again the phantom city burns;
And down the red-hot valley, lo!
The phantom armies marching go!

Blinking embers, tell me true,
Where are those armies marching to,
And what the burning city is,
That crumbles in your furnaces!

文爱艺 译

炉火中的军队

闪烁的灯光沿街而亮，
脚步发出细微的声响；
碧蓝的天空渐渐褪色，
花园的树木和墙逐渐模糊。

现在，幽暗的夜色渐渐降临，
火红的烛火映照空荡的屋子：
光芒让屋顶显得如此温暖，
火光跳跃在书脊上。

穿过城楼和高塔，
军队在烈火中行进，
直到我目不转睛地凝视，
军队才消失，光泽也随之渐弱。

然后光亮再一次回归，
幻城重燃那烈焰，
向着炽热的山谷，
幻影军队依旧前行！

闪烁的灰烬哪，快告诉我真相，
这些军队行进何方，
这燃烧着的又是哪座城市，
——在你的熔炉里崩溃粉碎！

THE LITTLE LAND

When at home alone I sit
And am very tired of it,
I have just to shut my eyes
To go sailing through the skies—
To go sailing far away
To the pleasant Land of Play;
To the fairy land afar
Where the Little People are;
Where the clover—tops are trees,
And the rain-pools are the seas,
And the leaves like little ships
Sail about on tiny trips;
And above the daisy tree
Through the grasses,
High o'erhead the Bumble Bee
Hums and passes.

In that forest to and fro
I can wander, I can go;
See the spider and the fly,
And the ants go marching by
Carrying parcels with their feet

小人国

每当我独自呆坐在家里，
十分厌倦这样的时光时，
我会闭上双眼，
去天空翱翔。
飞到很远很远的地方，
那里是嬉戏玩耍的乐园；
飞到远方的仙境，
那里是小人们的家园。
那儿，三叶草就是大树，
下雨的水塘就是海洋，
树叶，就是小舟，
来来回回，四处游荡；
在雏菊树上，
穿过草地，
还有大黄蜂在头顶上，
飞驶而过，嗡嗡作响。

在那片森林里，
我可以来去自如，
看到蜘蛛和苍蝇飞来飞去，
蚂蚁们列队前进，
用它们的双脚搬运包裹，

Down the green and grassy street.

I can in the sorrel sit

Where the ladybird alit.

I can climb the jointed grass;

And on high

See the greater swallows pass

In the sky,

And the round sun rolling by

Heeding no such things as I.

Through that forest I can pass

Till, as in a looking glass,

Humming fly and daisy tree

And my tiny self I see,

Painted very clear and neat

On the rain-pool at my feet.

Should a leaflet come to land

Drifting near to where I stand,

Straight I'll board that tiny boat

Round the rain-pool sea to float.

Little thoughtful creatures sit

On the grassy coasts of it;

Little things with lovely eyes

See me sailing with surprise.

文爱艺 译

穿过绿树成荫的街道。

我可以坐在草地上，

那儿瓢虫正萦绕，

我可以爬上草堆，

爬得高高的，

看大雁飞舞着，

在天空掠过，

落日滚滚而下，

不会注意到像我这样的小东西。

穿越那片森林，

直到，像是透过一面镜子，

飞蛾嗡嗡还有雏菊花儿树，

还看得见小小的我，

多么干净，多么整洁，

倒映在我脚边的雨塘中。

要是有一片小树叶飘落，

落在我驻足的地方，

我会立即登上那艘小船，

在雨池的海洋里四处游荡。

小小的思考者坐在一旁，

在海岸边的绿草地上，

睁着那可爱的眼睛，

惊讶地注视着我远航。

能唤起人们童年

美好回忆和情感的诗集

Some are clad in armor green —
(These have sure to battle been!) —
Some are pied with ev'ry hue,
Black and crimson, gold and blue;
Some have wings and swift are gone; —
But they all look kindly on.

When my eyes I once again
Open, And see all things plain:
High bare walls, great bare floor;
Great big knobs on drawer and door;
Great big people perched on chairs,
Stitching tucks and mending tears,
Each a hill that I could climb,
And talking nonsense all the time —

O dear me,
That I could be
A sailor on the rain—pool sea,
A climber in the clover tree,
And just come back, a sleepy-head,
Late at night to go to bed.

有些用绿草盔甲全副武装——
（它们肯定蓄势待发，准备作战！）——
有些被打扮得花花绿绿，
黑色和绯红，金黄色和碧蓝；
有些貊拍翅膀，迅速地飞走；——
但它们依旧有着友善的目光。

当我的眼睛再次睁开，
看到一切都很平常：
高处的围墙，宽广的地面，
大大的把手依然长在抽屉和大门上；
椅子上坐着正正经经的大人们，
缝着衣褶，补着衣裳，
每一个衣褶都像我攀爬的小山，
不停地唠唠叨叨——

哦，天哪，
我多想成为
一个池塘的水手，
一个三叶草树的攀登者，
贪睡虫却召唤我回来，
夜深了，我也要睡去了。

Garden Days

花园里的时光

昼与夜

当精彩的一天结束，
穿越关闭的天门，
孩童和花园，花朵和太阳。
世间的万物都将不见。

当迷糊的影子降临，
当光线逐渐消失，
在夜色的笼罩下，渐渐地，
全都消失。

花园黯淡下来，雏菊收拢花瓣，
孩童躺在床上，酣酣睡去——
萤火虫一如既往地停在公路的车辙上，
老鼠则躲在杂物堆里。

在黑暗中房子发出亮光，
父母亲拿着蜡烛来回走动；
直到，神圣的夜，
转开卧室的门把手。

终于白天来临，
东方破晓，
在树篱枝头，金雀花巅，
沉睡的鸟儿也醒来了。

在黑暗中万物的形状，

房子、树木、树篱，
变得越来越清晰；还有麻雀的翅膀，
在窗台上拍打。

文觉艺 译

这会惊醒打哈欠的奴仆；
她会打开园门——
看到园中空地的露珠，
清晨就来临了。

我的花园重又生机勃勃，
涂上了绿色和玫瑰色，
正像是夜晚他们从我的玻璃窗后
消失了一样新奇。

就像玩具一样，
它们被夜晚关了起来，
我看见它们在白天重放光芒，
在明亮的天际下。

露珠安心酣睡，
在每一条小径每一块田地，
每一丛玫瑰，
每一株蓝色勿忘我上。

"起来！"它们喊叫，"白天来了！"
在微笑的山谷，
我们已经敲响清晨的鼓点。
"伙伴们，来加入你们的队列吧！"

能唤起人们童年
美好回忆和情感的诗集

NIGHT AND DAY

When the golden day is done,
Through the closing portal,
Child and garden, flower and sun,
Vanish all things mortal.

As the blinding shadows fall,
As the rays diminish,
Under evening's cloak, they all
Roll away and vanish.

Garden darkened, daisy shut,
Child in bed, they slumber—
Glowworm in the highway rut,
Mice among the lumber.

In the darkness houses shine,
Parents move the candles;
Till on all the night divine
Turns the bedroom handles.

Till at last the day begins
In the east a-breaking,
In the hedges and the whins
Sleeping birds a-waking.

In the darkness shapes of things,

Houses, trees, and hedges,
Clearer grow; and sparrow's wings
Beat on window ledges.

These shall wake the yawning maid;
She the door shall open—
Finding dew on garden glade
And the morning broken.

There my garden grows again
Green and rosy painted,
As at eve behind the pane
From my eyes it fainted.

Just as it was shut away,
Toy-like, in the even,
Here I see it glow with day
Under glowing heaven.

Every path and every plot,
Every bush of roses,
Every blue forget-me-not
Where the dew reposes,

"Up!" they cry, "the day is come!"
On the smiling valleys;
We have beat the morning drum;
"Playmate, join your allies!"

文爱艺 译

能唤起人们童年

美好回忆和情感的诗集

鸟巢中的蛋

阳光明媚的日子，
鸟儿们都叽叽喳喳地叫个不停，
栖身在月桂树枝
编织的帐篷里。

在树杈间，
有一个褐色的鸟巢，
鸟妈妈耐心地
孵着那四个小小的蓝色鸟蛋。

我们就在旁边看着，
像傻子一样看着，
每一个鸟蛋里面
都安全地住着一只鸟宝宝。

不久蛋壳就会被啄碎，

文爱艺　译

鸟儿们争从高中歌唱，
让四月的森林
变成歌声的海洋。

它们比我们还小，
啊孩子，比我们还柔弱，
不久后在蔚蓝的空中，
它们将是——
歌手和水手。

我们年纪比它们大，
也长得高得多壮得多，
却不能再像这样小瞧，
鸟儿宝宝。

它们将伴着歌声
振翅高飞
高高飞过，
山毛榉林的上空。

尽管我们很聪明，
也伶牙俐齿，
我们却只能用双脚，
缓慢地前行。

能唤起人们童年
美好回忆和情感的诗集

NEST EGGS

Birds all the sunny day
Flutter and quarrel
Here in the arbor-like
Tent of the laurel.

Here in the fork
The brown nest is seated;
Four little blue eggs
The mother keeps heated.

While we stand watching her,
Staring like gabies,
Safe in each egg are the
Bird's little babies.

Soon the frail eggs they shall
Chip, and up springing
Make all the April woods
Merry with singing.

Younger than we are,
O children, and frailer,

文爱艺 译

Soon in blue air they'll be,
　　Singer and sailor.

We, so much older,
　　Taller and stronger,
We shall look down on the
　　Birdies no longer.

They shall go flying
With musical speeches
High overhead in the
Tops of the beeches.

In spite of our wisdom
And sensible talking,
We on our feet must go
Plodding and walking.

花儿

保姆告诉我你们的名字：
园丁的吊袜带，牧羊人的钱包，
单身汉的纽扣，女士的罩衫；
还有女士蜀葵。

童话的境地，神奇的生灵，
梦幻的森林里野蜂飞舞，
小树下藏着仙女——
这些肯定都是仙国里的名字。

还有小树林——在树枝底下
精灵编织了一个家。
小小的树梢上，玫瑰或百里香，
勇敢的精灵在上面攀爬！

大人们种的树林很美丽，
但最神奇的森林还数这里；
如果我不是长得那么高，
我完全可以在那儿好好地生活。

文爱艺 译

THE FLOWERS

All the names I know from nurse:
Gardener's garters, Shepherd's purse,
Bachelor's buttons, Lady's smock,
And the Lady Hollyhock.

Fairy places, fairy things,
Fairy woods where the wild bee wings,
Tiny trees for tiny dames —
These must all be fairy names!

Tiny woods below whose boughs
Shady fairies weave a house;
Tiny treetops, rose or thyme,
Where the braver fairies climb!

Fair are grown-up people's trees,
But the fairest woods are these;
Where, if I were not so tall,
I should live for good and all.

能唤起人们童年
美好回忆和情感的诗集

夏日骄阳

壮丽的太阳，普照大地，
穿越空旷的苍穹，不眠不息。
在晴空万里、骄阳似火的日子里，
喷洒着比雨丝还密的光线。

虽然我们把窗帘拉得严严实实，
让房间保持凉爽，
然而他还是会搜到一两道缝隙，
让他的金色手指悄悄地溜进来。

蜘蛛网爬满了灰扑扑的阁楼，
他，却能穿过钥匙孔，轻轻松松；
透过破旧砖瓦的边缘，
笑眯眯地钻进架着梯子的干草棚。

同时，他总是挂着灿烂的微笑，
洒满花园的每一处角落，
透露着深情的目光，
照射到常青藤最最隐蔽的角落。

穿过山峦，跨越大海，
永不停息地照耀着灿烂的天空，
取悦孩子，给玫瑰上色，
他是世间的园丁，普照大地。

文爱艺 译

SUMMER SUN

Great is the sun, and wide he goes
Through empty heaven without repose;
And in the blue and glowing days
More thick than rain he showers his rays.

Though closer still the blinds we pull
To keep the shady parlor cool,
Yet he will find a chink or two
To slip his golden fingers through.

The dusty attic spider-clad
He, through the keyhole, maketh glad;
And through the broken edge of tiles,
Into the laddered hayloft smiles.

Meantime his golden face around
He bares to all the garden ground,
And sheds a warm and glittering look
Among the ivy's inmost nook.

Above the hills, along the blue,
Round the bright air with footing true,
To please the child, to paint the rose,
The gardener of the World, he goes.

能唤起人们童年
美好回忆和情感的诗集

沉默的士兵

草地刚修剪过，
我独自在草坪上行走，
在一块草皮上，我发现了一个小洞，
把一个兵藏在这洞中。

春天来了，雏菊盛开；
绿草掩盖了我的秘密圣地；
草地上的波浪像绿色的海洋，
高低起伏，涌向我的膝盖。

在绿草下，他一个人躺着，
目光呆滞，仰望苍天，
绯红色的衣裳，上膛的枪，
望着星空和骄阳。

当绿草如谷物般成熟时，
当长柄大镰刀再次扫过时，
当草地被修剪整齐，
我的小洞会再次出现。

我就能找到他，不用担心，
我会找到我的掷弹兵；

不管一切如何改变，
我会发现我的沉默的士兵。

这个小东西曾经活在
春天茂密的森林里；
如果他能告诉我真相，
那正是我向往的生活。

他见过星星闪耀的夜晚，
欣赏过春天美丽的鲜花；
还有那些在森林的草丛中
匆匆飞过的小精灵。

在沉默中他听过
蜜蜂和瓢虫的窃窃私语，
当他孤独地躺着的时候，
还有蝴蝶在他的头顶飞舞。

他一个字也不会说，
也不懂人类的语言。
我必须把他搁在架子上，
然后自己编织故事。

THE DUMB SOLDIER

When the grass was closely mown,
Walking on the lawn alone,
In the turf a hole I found,
And hid a soldier underground.

Spring and daisies came apace;
Grasses hide my hiding place;
Grasses run like a green sea
O'er the lawn up to my knee.

Under grass alone he lies,
Looking up with leaden eyes,
Scarlet coat and pointed gun,
To the stars and to the sun.

When the grass is ripe like grain,
When the scythe is stoned again,
When the lawn is shaven clear,
Then my hole shall reappear.

I shall find him, never fear,
I shall find my grenadier;

文爱艺 译

But for all that's gone and come,
I shall find my soldier dumb.

He has lived, a little thing,
In the grassy woods of spring;
Done, if he could tell me true,
Just as I should like to do.

He has seen the starry hours
And the springing of the flowers;
And the fairy things that pass
In the forests of the grass.

In the silence he has heard
Talking bee and ladybird,
And the butterfly has flown
O'er him as he lay alone.

Not a word will he disclose,
Not a word of all he knows.
I must lay him on the shelf,
And make up the tale myself.

秋之火

其他的花园
都在高高的山谷上，
看秋日的篝火
划出一阵阵烟火！

美好的夏天过去了，
所有的夏花也随之凋谢，
通红的火焰熊熊燃烧，
灰暗的烟儿高高地飘扬。

唱首季节歌吧！
明朗轻快的！
夏日的花儿，
秋天的烟火！

138 / 139

文爱艺 译

AUTUMN FIRES

In the other gardens
And all up the vale,
From the Autumn bonfires
See the smoke trail!

Pleasant Summer over
And all the Summer flowers,
The red fire blazes,
The gray smoke towers.

Sing a song of seasons!
Something bright in all!
Flowers in the Summer,
Fires in the Fall!

能唤起人们童年
美好回忆和情感的诗集

园丁

这个园丁不爱说话，
他让我沿着鹅卵石道散步；
当他收起工具时
他会锁上门，带走钥匙。

在那排醋栗后面，
除了厨师没人会经过，
在远远的地里，我看到他在挖洞，
苍老而又严肃，皮肤黝黑身材高大。

他挖了些花儿，有绿的、红的，还有蓝的，
也不想跟人讲话。
他挖了些花儿，又除了些草，
他从来都不会想着去玩耍。

傻园丁啊，夏天走了，
冬天悄悄来临，
当花园仅剩枯枝藤条，
你也该放下你的推车。

然而现在，夏日正酣，
该好好利用这大好时光，
你要是跟我玩印度大战
将会变得更加聪明！

文爱艺 译

THE GARDENER

The gardener does not love to talk,
He makes me keep the gravel walk;
And when he puts his tools away,
He locks the door and takes the key.

Away behind the currant row
Where no one else but cook may go,
Far in the plots, I see him dig,
Old and serious, brown and big.

He digs the flowers, green, red, and blue,
Nor wishes to be spoken to.
He digs the flowers and cuts the hay,
And never seems to want to play.

Silly gardener! Summer goes,
And Winter comes with pinching toes,
When in the garden bare and brown
You must lay your barrow down.

Well now, and while the Summer stays,
To profit by these garden days,
O how much wiser you would be
To play at Indian wars with me!

能唤起人们童年
美好回忆和情感的诗集

历史畅想

亲爱的吉姆叔叔，
现在你正抽着烟斗，在花园里闲逛。
可知这花园经历了多少不朽的事迹，
有失败也有胜利的英勇斗争。

我们最好踮起脚，
这样走路我们才会安全，
因为这是个被施了魔法的地方，
谁在这儿闲逛，谁就会陷入沉睡。

这儿是大海，这儿是沙滩，
这儿是纯朴的牧羊人的国土，
这是美丽的蜀葵丛，
那是阿里巴巴的礁石。

可是你瞧！远处的高地上，
西伯利亚冰天雪地，我
还有罗伯特·布鲁斯和威廉·泰尔
被巫师的魔法困在那里。

在那儿，我们被囚禁，
冰冷的地牢不见天日；
但终于，我们拼尽全力，冲了出去，
挣脱那铁打的脚镣。

全城的号角都响起，

文爱艺 译

所有的城门都关闭，
巨人们纷纷跳上马背，
穿过灌木林，向我们紧逼。

我和我的同伴们，马不停蹄，
翻越青山，跨过银河，
渡过澎湃大海，
穿过塔塔里的橡胶林。

我们飞奔了上千里，
穿过女巫的小路，
挥舞着无敌的利剑，
我们冲过要塞，直抵中原。

最后，我们拉住缰绳——
我们三个已经筋疲力尽，
在草坪上，该是喝茶的光景。
我们跳下战马，
站在巴比伦王国的城门下。

能唤起人们童年

美好回忆和情感的诗集

HISTORICAL ASSOCIATIONS

Dear Uncle Jim, this garden ground
That now you smoke your pipe around,
Has seen immortal actions done
And valiant battles lost and won.

Here we had best on tiptoe tread,
While I for safety march ahead,
For this is that enchanted ground
Where all who loiter slumber sound.

Here is the sea, here is the sand,
Here is simple Shepherd's Land,
Here are the fairy hollyhocks,
And there are Ali Baba's rocks.

But yonder, see! apart and high,
Frozen Siberia lies; where I,
With Robert Bruce and William Tell,
Was bound by an enchanter's spell.

There, then, awhile in chains we lay,
In wintry dungeons, far from day;

文爱艺 译

But ris'n at length, with might and main,
Our iron fetters burst in twain.

Then all the horns were blown in town;
And to the ramparts clanging down,
All the giants leaped to horse
And charged behind us through the gorse.

On we rode, the others and I,
Over the mountains blue, and by
The Silver River, the sounding sea,
And the robber woods of Tartary.

A thousand miles we galloped fast,
And down the witches'lane we passed,
And rode amain with brandished sword,
Up to the middle, through the ford.

Last we drew rein—a weary three—
Upon the lawn, in time for tea,
And from our steeds alighted down
Before the gates of Babylon.

能唤起人们童年
美好回忆和情感的诗集

ENVOYS

使者

致威利和汉丽塔

如果两个人能够读懂
这些旧日欢乐的时光
在房屋和花园中的嬉闹，
我的表兄妹们，只有你们，可能做到。

你们在郁郁葱葱的花园里
和我一起，扮演国王，王后，
猎人，士兵，和水手，
还有好多好多，专属孩子的乐趣。

现如今，我们是长辈了，
我们正襟危坐，
透过窗户的边沿
看着孩子们，我们的后代们，在玩耍。

"时光啊！"老年人感叹
飞逝不可逆转；
没有人能挽留时光，
当它匆匆飞逝，留下的是无限的爱。

TO WILLIE AND HENRIETTA

If two may read aright
These rhymes of old delight
And house and garden play,
You two, my cousins, and you only, may.

You in a garden green
With me were king and queen,
Were hunter, soldier, tar,
And all the thousand things that children are.

Now in the elders' seat
We rest with quiet feet,
And from the window—bay
We watch the children, our successors, play.

"Time was." the golden head
Irrevocably said;
But time which none can bind,
While flowing fast away, leaves love behind.

致母亲

我的母亲，也来读读我的诗吧，
为了那爱意满满的难忘时光，
您也许还会有机会再次听到
我在地板上的脚步声。

TO MY MOTHER

You too, my mother,
read my rhymes
For love of unforgotten times,
And you may chance to hear once more
The little feet along the floor.

A Child's Garden of Verses

致阿姨

院长阿姨——不单单是我，
所有您照料过的孩童都很好奇——
其他的孩子是怎么过的？
没有您，我们的童年将会怎样？

文爱艺 译

TO AUNTIE

Chief of our aunts — not only I,

But all your dozen of nurslings cry —

What did the other children do?

And what were childhood, wanting you?

能唤起人们童年美好回忆和情感的诗集

写给我的孩子

1

小路易斯·桑切斯，如果你以适当的进度学习，
　　总有一天，你就会读到这本诗集，
　　然后，你将发现，很久之前，你的名字
　　　被伦敦的英国书商印在了书上。

　　在这个喧嚣的大城市，东西方文化交会之地，
　　　所有这些小小的字母都用英文印刷。
　　然而你什么也不用想，因为你还小，不能玩耍，
　　　异国的人们在很远很远的地方想着你。

　　当你入睡时，我的宝贝，在英伦各个岛屿上
　　　其他的小孩儿会捧起这本诗集，
　　他们疑惑着，在他们自己的家里，在海的另一边：
　　这个小路易斯到底是谁，妈妈请你告诉我，好吗？

文爱艺 译

2

既然你已经学完了你的课程，放下诗集玩去吧，
到蒙特里海滩上寻找贝壳和海藻，
看那巨大的鲸须被微风掩埋，
小小的矶鹞，大大的太平洋。

记得玩耍时会有海雾滚滚而来，在你能读懂之前，
我该如何告诉你怎么做，当你谁也不想时，
可知在几乎半个世界那么远的地方，
会有某个人在蒙特里海滩将路易斯深深想念！

能唤起人们童年
美好回忆和情感的诗集

TO MY NAME-CHILD

1

Some day soon this rhyming volume, if you learn with proper speed,
Little Louis Sanchez, will be given you to read.
Then you shall discover, that your name was printed down
By the English printers, long before, in London town.

In the great and busy city where the East and West are met,
All the little letters did the English printer set;
While you thought of nothing, and were still too young to play,
Foreign people thought of you In places far away.

Ay, and while you slept, a baby, over all the English lands
Other little children took the volume in their hands;
Other children questioned, in their homes across the seas:
Who was little Louis, won't you tell us, mother, please?

2

Now that you have spelt your lesson, lay it down and go and play,
Seeking shells and seaweed on the sands of Monterey,
Watching all the mighty whalebones, lying buried by the breeze,
Tiny sandpipers, and the huge Pacific seas.

And remember in your playing, as the sea-fog rolls to you,
Long ere you could read it, how I told you what to do;
And that while you thought of no one, nearly half the world away
Some one thought of Louis on the beach of Monterey!

致米妮

红屋子里有张巨大的床
那儿只让年长的人躺；
你和我曾经一同躺过的小屋
我曾牵你的手郑重求婚
那是育婴所里最美好的日子
墙上贴满了照片；
还有百叶窗上的树叶，
从一个舒适的房间醒来
听见花园里的树叶在摇晃——
在风中沙沙作响

多么幸福啊，舒服地躺在床上
看着头顶上的图片——

文双艺 译

有关塞瓦斯托波尔的战争

依墙而靠的裸露的枪支——

无畏地登梯攻城，

疾驰的船只，咩咩叫的羊群，

膝盖高的快乐孩童

行走时咯咯欢笑：

所有的一切都消失得干干净净，

就连古老的牧师住宅如今也已改变；

看不明白的神情

露出完全陌生的面孔。

河流，流经一个个磨坊，

仍然会经过我们儿时的花园；

但是，啊，我们不再是孩童了

应该在水门上看清这一点！

下面的紫杉——它依旧在那里——

似乎那清脆的声音还在空中回响

就像是我们还在玩耍，

我能听得到他们的呼叫和交谈：

"去巴比伦有多远？"

啊，很远很远，亲爱的，

很远，离这儿很远——

但是你还可以走得更远！

"烛光能引领我走到那儿吗？"

正如旧诗句所说的。

我不知道——也许你能——

只是也许 ，孩子们，听仔细了。

啊，不要再回来了！

永恒的黎明，毫无疑问，

定会在山丘和平原破晓，

隐去所有的星星，熄灭所有的蜡烛

在这之前我们会返老还童。

致远在印度的你，这些

我越洋寄给你，

不要觉得它太遥远。

因为那些我们早已忘记，还有印度橱柜

羚羊的骨头，信天翁的翅膀，

穿着彩色花衣的鸟儿和豌豆，

帆船和镯子，珠帘子和屏风，

圣父和神圣的钟声，

还有螺纹贝壳的嗡嗡响声？

客厅地板的水平线

就像忠诚、朴实的苏格兰海岸；

但是当我们爬上椅子时，

瞧哇，神圣的东方就在那儿！

这是个传说，看吧

我就在客厅里，老态龙钟，

文爱艺 译

米妮就在我的上方

摆在古色古香的印度橱柜内，

友好地微笑着，使书橱熠熠生辉

太高了，我自己够不到。

伸出一只手，亲爱的，然后伴着

这些旋律，纪念我们曾相识一场。

能唤起人们童年

美好回忆和情感的诗集

TO MINNIE

The red room with the giant bed
Where none but elders laid their head;
The little room where you and I
Did for awhile together lie
And, simple suitor, I your hand
In decent marriage did demand;
The great day nursery, best of all,
With pictures pasted on the wall
And leaves upon the blind —
A pleasant room wherein to wake
And hear the leafy garden shake
And rustle in the wind —

And pleasant there to lie in bed
And see the pictures overhead —
The wars about Sebastopol,
The grinning guns along the wall,
The daring escalade,
The plunging ships, the bleating sheep,

文爱艺　译

The happy children ankle-deep

And laughing as they wade:

All these are vanished clean away,

And the old manse is changed today;

It wears an altered face

And shields a stranger race.

The river, on from mill to mill,

Flows past our childhood's garden still;

But ah! we children never more

Shall watch it from the water-door!

Below the yew — it still is there —

Our phantom voices haunt the air

As we were still at play,

And I can hear them call and say:

"How far is it to Babylon?"

Ah, far enough, my dear,

Far, far enough from here —

Yet you have farther gone!

"Can I get there by candlelight?"

So goes the old refrain.

I do not know — perchance you might —

But only, children, hear it right,

能唤起人们童年

美好回忆和情感的诗集

A Child's Garden of Verses

Ah, never to return again!
The eternal dawn, beyond a doubt,
Shall break on hill and plain,
And put all stars and candles out,
Ere we be young again.

To you in distant India, these
I send across the seas,
Nor count it far across.
For which of us forgets
The Indian cabinets,
The bones of antelope, the wings of albatross,
The pied and painted birds and beans,
The junks and bangles, beads and screens,
The gods and sacred bells,
And the loud-humming, twisted shells?

The level of the parlor floor
Was honest, homely, Scottish shore;
But when we climbed upon a chair,
Behold the gorgeous East was there!
Be this a fable; and behold
Me in the parlor as of old,
And Minnie just above me set
In the quaint Indian cabinet!

文爱艺　译

Smiling and kind, you grace a shelf

Too high for me to reach myself.

Reach down a hand, my dear, and take

These rhymes for old acquaintance' sake.

致读者

TO ANY READER

As from the house your mother sees
You playing round the garden trees,
So you may see, if you will look
Through the windows of this book,
Another child, far, far away,
And in another garden, play.
But do not think you can at all,
By knocking on the window, call
That child to hear you. His intent
Is all on his play-business bent.

He does not hear; he will not look,
Nor yet be lured out of this book.
For, long ago, the truth to say,
He has grown up and gone away,
And it is but a child of air
That lingers in the garden there.

文爱艺 译

致读者

如同妈妈从房里看到

你在花园的树丛中玩闹，

如果你把这本小书当作一扇窗户，

你同样可看到，在很远很远的地方，

有一个小孩儿在另一个花园里，也在玩闹。

但永远不要奢望，

轻叩那扇窗，呼唤他，

他就能听到你。

他只想自己玩耍。

他听不到你的呼唤，看不到你的存在，

他也不会被书外的世界吸引。

因为，事实上在很久很久以前，

他长大了，然后离去，

只剩孩童般的稚气

留在了儿童诗园，久久不忍离去。

能唤起人们童年

美好回忆和情感的诗集